Zoë
and the
Wishing Star

To Rachael

First published in Great Britain in 2008
by Piccadilly Press Ltd,
5 Castle Road, London NW1 8PR
www.piccadillypress.co.uk

Text designed by Louise Millar
Colour reproduction by Dot Gradations Ltd UK
Printed and bound in China by WKT

ISBN: 978 1 85340 988 2 (hardback)
978 1 85340 987 5 (paperback)

1 3 5 7 9 10 8 6 4 2

A catalogue record of this book
is available from the British Library

Jane Andrews lives in Winnelie, Australia with her husband. She has two sons.
Piccadilly Press also publish the other books in this series:

ISBN: 978 1 85340 651 5 (p/b)

ISBN: 978 1 85340 644 7 (p/b)

ISBN: 978 1 85340 726 0 (p/b)

ISBN: 978 1 85340 728 4 (p/b)

ISBN: 978 1 85340 744 4 (p/b)

ISBN: 978 1 85340 816 8 (p/b)

ISBN: 978 1 85340 838 0 (p/b)

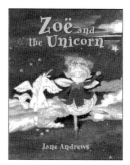

ISBN: 978 1 85340 915 8 (p/b)

Zoë
and the
Wishing Star

Jane Andrews

Piccadilly Press • London

Zoë and Pip were working very hard in the Fairy Queen's garden. They were so busy they didn't realise how late it was.

As darkness fell, they saw the most beautiful star shining brightly down at them.
"Look, Pip! It's the Wishing Star! It means that someone in the human world is making a wish and we can help them."

Suddenly a strong gust of wind lifted
Zoë and Pip into the air with a *whoosh*
and blew them over fairy land . . .

. . . and into a little girl's bedroom!

"I wish I had a cat," the little girl was saying
as she looked at the Wishing Star.

Just then her mother came in. "Are you still wishing for a cat, Katrina?" she asked kindly.

"It's a shame we can't have one. This flat is on the top floor, and cats like to go outside. We don't have the money to feed one, either."

As Katrina slept, the two fairies tried to find a cat which didn't eat very much and liked to stay indoors.

"No, thank you," purred two sleek fat cats in a house nearby. "We are far too comfortable to move."

"Oh no, we love being outside all the time," hissed the alley cats.

Zoë and Pip looked everywhere, but they couldn't find a cat for Katrina anywhere.

Zoë and Pip were so tired that they rested on
the fence outside Katrina's block of flats.
"What can we do now?" sighed Pip.

Just then, Zoë nudged Pip and pointed to the ground
floor flat. There was a cat, staring out of the window.
"It looks very sad," said Pip, as they flew down and
tapped on the window.

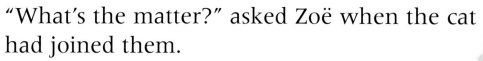

"What's the matter?" asked Zoë when the cat
had joined them.
"I am so lonely," replied the cat. "I love my
owner and she feeds me well, but she is too
old to play with me very much."

Zoë and Pip looked at each other.
"Leave it to us!" said Zoë. "We can help you!"

The next day, Zoë hovered over Katrina and
her mother as they left the block of flats.

And Pip hovered over the old lady and
the cat as they sat in the garden.
Then they both waved their wands and . . .

Ping!

Katrina smiled at the cat, and the cat
leapt down and nuzzled against her.

Her mother smiled at the old lady and sat down beside her.

And soon everyone had made a new friend!

When Zoë and Pip saw the Wishing Star
that evening, they knew it had come to
take them home.
The Fairy Queen and their friends were
waiting for them in the fairy garden.

"Well done!" said the Fairy Queen, when she heard their story. "The Wishing Star told me how hard you worked to make the little girl's wish come true."

And Zoë and Pip were very proud. Once again they
had used their magic to make someone happy.